PLEASE STAY

STONE TWINS DUET BOOK 1

TONI DENISE

1
____

rcher climbed out of the pool and grabbed his white-and-blue towel from the chair, quickly wiping off his face. Taking the towel over his head, he dried out his hair some and draped the towel over the chair before sitting down on it.

He'd been doing laps in the pool before his brother, Austin, and Austin's girlfriend, Victoria, came outside. Looking over at the couple, he couldn't help the jealousy he felt at their happiness.

They looked exactly the same, Archer and Austin, both over six feet tall, both with sandy-blond hair that they styled differently, but had the same haircut. Both of them preferred a little length in their hair. They were both tanned, courtesy of the time spent at the pool and the beach.

Archer had tattoos, of course. He couldn't think of a more appropriate way to tell them apart than the tattoos. Archer had covered his chest and back with ink and was starting on his arms. Austin was every bit the straitlaced banker with no tattoos and, despite Archer's urging, no plans to have any.

The only thing different about them was the way their brains worked. Archer had always been the dark to Austin's light, with very few exceptions. Austin was the perfect twin, and Archer, well he struggled with basic things, like reading.

His parents had been distraught when his grades weren't good. His father had completely written him off at the mere mention of dyslexia, as though it somehow prevented him from being able to do anything. He could do it; it just took more effort, effort he didn't put into things because no one seemed to care.

It wasn't all terrible. He and Austin lived together now, not too far from where they'd grown up. Rather than do anything productive, as his father would say, Archer had taken to art and sculpting, particularly with metal. Something about bending everything to his will made him feel powerful and actually eased a lot of his stress.

Austin had gone corporate and was being prepped to take over his father's banking business. There was no jealousy at that prospect. Archer had no interest in finances outside of his own. Austin had what he always wanted though: that steady relationship with a girl that seemed to understand him.

He slipped on his sunglasses as he laid back in his chair, taking in the couple that was across from him. Victoria sat on Austin's lap, as she always did. Her bleach-blonde hair was perfectly straightened, a million products in it, he was sure.

She wouldn't get in the pool; he knew that. That also meant that Austin wouldn't get in either. Archer had splashed her once, and they'd both gotten upset with him. It had turned into a bad night. He didn't understand being so high-maintenance that you wouldn't enjoy the water.

He continued to watch them as they chatted, completely

oblivious to him out there as well. He wanted that. The person that was so into you, that understood you so well, that you forgot the world around you.

Archer had trouble communicating, always had. He thought things through differently than everyone else, and that made it hard for people to understand him, and apparently for him to understand them. Victoria was one of the few women he could talk to and that understood him, probably just from being forced to be around him for three years now.

Girlfriends had come and gone in his life, none of them lasting more than a month or two. They had a friend, Rachel, that they'd known since they were children, that completely understood him, better than even Austin did. It was nice having her around most times, but he wanted a relationship like Austin and Victoria.

"What's the dinner plans for tonight?" Archer yelled across the pool.

"We were thinking of grilling some chicken," Austin yelled back.

"How about steak?" It was always only chicken or fish with Victoria over. She had to keep up with her diet of course, one he wasn't interested in participating in.

Austin said something to Victoria, and she got up, laughing. She waited for him to stand and then took the seat he'd been in before. Austin made his way around the pool to Archer.

"You know she doesn't eat red meat, man," Austin told him as he approached.

"She's here almost every day now, man. I'm tired of chicken and salads," Archer complained.

"Me too," Austin admitted. "How about tomorrow night? We can do steaks and invite Rachel over too?"

Rachel and Victoria were not friends. They faked it, but it was so painfully obvious that the nice was fake, sometimes it hurt to watch. He didn't understand their issue. Rachel thought Victoria was manipulative, but he didn't see it, and neither did Austin.

"Sounds like a plan. Where's she gonna be?"

"Some fancy dinner with her parents." Austin made a face that told him he wasn't interested in going.

"Better her than us." Archer laughed.

"Agreed. You reach out to Rachel?"

"Yeah, I'll let her know."

That was one problem that happened often. Austin never used his phone to talk to Rachel. Victoria would get mad, saying that Rachel was trying to cause problems in their relationship. It was one of the only things he didn't like about her. It was likely insecurity, but it was ridiculous.

"Thanks." Austin stood. "You eating with us tonight then?"

"Absolutely not. I'll grab a burger."

"Sneak me some fries?" Austin raised his eyebrows.

"You could just eat them in front of her."

"Nah, not worth it."

"Fries are always worth it," Archer told him seriously.

"Shut up."

"I'm going to the studio. I'll be back late probably." Archer stood too, grabbing his towel.

"See you later then."

They did a handshake that ended in a brief one-armed hug that they'd done forever, and Archer left the pool, not looking back. He let himself into the kitchen, heading straight for the stairs and his room. He needed to get out of the house and hopefully work off some frustration in the studio.

2

---

*R*achel let herself into her house and locked the door behind her. She was exhausted after that workout. She tossed her purple leggings and sports bra onto the floor as she headed for the shower.

She told herself constantly that she wouldn't need to work out so hard if she would just eat better, but she loved food, so it was the price she had to pay. Smiling, she considered what she was going to have for dinner tonight. Surely she'd earned something greasy with that workout.

After her shower she quickly got dressed in a comfortable pair of pajama shorts and a loose T-shirt before throwing her shoulder-length brown hair into a ponytail to keep it out of the way. Settling on the sofa, her phone buzzed before she could start searching for delivery places.

Dinner at our house tomorrow?

She stared back at the text from Archer, debating how to answer. She'd love to go but was so tired of dealing with Victoria. The backhanded compliments were getting to her, and she wasn't in the mood for the nonsense. She didn't want to directly ask if she would be there either.

Please? It's just me and Austin.

As though reading her mind, Archer had answered her question before she even asked it. She couldn't help the smile that spread across her face. She loved that he would be able to do that.

Sure, want me to bring anything?

Swimsuit?

What are we eating?

STEAK

He emphasized with all caps. It was unnecessary; she knew how excited that would make him without that hint.

See you then.

She answered him and then set her phone down. It had been a while since they'd all hung out. Lately, she'd avoided hanging out with them because of Victoria.

It was three years that Victoria and Austin had been together, and at this point she figured they'd get married and Austin would never see Victoria for who she really was. She'd been manipulating both of them from the beginning, but it was masterful.

Everything Victoria wanted from them, she got it. She would make it so they wanted to do it for her, which meant that the one time Rachel had pointed it out to the Stone twins, they'd assured her they wanted to. It was insane, and she couldn't watch it anymore, so she'd been distancing herself.

She also liked Archer more than she should, and couldn't seem to make herself stop. She'd been close with both of them, but Archer had always had a hold over her that he didn't even realize. Not wanting to jeopardize their friendship and positive he was not interested in her as anything other than a friend, she'd never said anything to him about it, or anyone for that matter.

Archer had a rough relationship with his parents and had always come to Rachel over it. She'd helped as best as she could with him to cope. She'd done so much research on dyslexia to help Archer back in school. He wanted to do the work, just struggled, so she'd secretly helped him through high school.

Art had been his outlet, and she'd hung out at his rented studio more than she'd been at home after they graduated. She was there when he sold his first piece and was there when he'd hated the ones he was working on and would throw things across the studio in frustration.

She missed him. Tomorrow would be fun to hang out with them again. However, tonight wasn't going to be splurge night, since she knew that dinner at the Stones' would be carb heavy.

She stood and went to the kitchen, looking through the fridge. She pulled out a leftover container of some zucchini pasta she had made yesterday and set it on the counter. A knock on the door interrupted her. Confused, she went to see who was here.

Archer was smiling through the peephole when she checked, holding bags of food soaked in grease.

"What are you doing here?" she asked, opening the door wide to let him in.

"I was hungry." He shrugged as though this was where he ate.

"What if I wasn't home?" She followed him to the kitchen.

"Then I'd have more to eat."

The grin he gave her sent shivers through her. She took a steadying breath and looked through the bags. It was exactly what she had planned to get for herself before he texted: a greasy burger and fries.

She sighed and pulled the food out, putting it on the plates he'd already gotten.

"You're ruining my diet."

"You don't even like diets."

"Like and need are two different things."

He looked at the container on the counter, opening it. "This is not what you were going to eat tonight, right? How do you survive?" He made a face.

"Give it back, and yes, that's my dinner," she said defensively. Rachel didn't really want it either, but life was about checks and balances.

"Absolutely not." He held it high.

"Are you a child? I am not going to reach for it. I know good and well I can't reach that high, so give me my dinner." She folded her arms and glared at him.

"Your dinner is here." He gestured to the burgers and fries.

"I can't eat that tonight if I am coming over to eat tomorrow," she told him.

"What is with the diet? That's not like you." He set the container down on the counter.

"I don't want to gain any more weight. I'm trying to eat better."

"One"—he held up his finger—"gain what weight?" He looked her up and down, "Two, what's the point of eating if it's not enjoyable?"

"You don't see the weight gain because you don't look at me. And eating is to survive?" She questioned his logic.

"Whatever, you do you. I'm not going to apologize for bringing you good food." He made his plate and carried it to her living room.

Rachel rolled her eyes. She didn't want him to think he

won that argument, but she really wanted the burger and fries instead of her cold fake pasta.

After only a moment's hesitation, she made her plate of burger and fries and joined Archer in the living room. He raised one eyebrow at her food choice but didn't say anything.

"I didn't want you to waste your money on dinner and let it go bad," she defended.

Archer choked on the french fry he had been chewing. "That's rich." He laughed between coughs.

3

———

"You invited her, right?" Austin asked as Archer pulled the steak off the grill.

"I did. She said she was coming." He was also worried she wasn't going to show.

"Well, call her and see where she is," Austin practically demanded.

"You call her."

"I can't, you know that, now come on."

Just then Rachel walked out onto the back deck. "Hey guys!" she said, holding a tray of food.

"You came!" Austin picked her up and spun her in a hug as soon as she set the tray down.

Laughing, Rachel hugged him back. Back on her feet again, she slapped him. "You're going to make me dizzy, and I almost dropped dessert."

"Dessert?" Archer lifted the foil on the tray to see brownies underneath. "Oh, my God, you made brownies?"

"I did."

"We've died and gone to heaven," Austin teased, pulling

the foil all the way back and picking one up, immediately taking a bite and moaning.

"Those are dessert!" Rachel fussed.

"Nontraditional around here: dessert first," Archer teased as he picked up a brownie as well.

The brownie was delicious, and he couldn't help but moan as his brother had. The gooey chocolate was exactly what he needed though he'd only just realized it.

"Whatever." She pouted. "Where's the real food?"

"Steaks are here. Austin is on sides," Archer reminded him.

"Shit! The macaroni!" Austin ran for the house, nearly falling over his own feet as he did.

"I turned it off when I came in." Rachel winked at him and took a seat.

"Did you bring your suit?" Archer asked. He was ready to go for a swim, thinking it would be better to eat after.

"I want dinner that I was promised."

"Later. Come on," he pleaded with her, knowing he would get his way.

"Fine," she said with a sigh, slipping her dress over her head, revealing her black bikini underneath.

"Damn, Rach, doing that swimsuit justice today, huh?" he teased.

"Shut up. I've gained ten pounds, and I didn't have another one to wear."

"Lies." She didn't look like she'd put on any weight. She may have been his friend, but he could appreciate a female body as much as the next man.

"You guys ready to eat?" Austin asked, carrying a pot to the table on the deck.

"We are swimming first." Archer gestured toward the pool.

The concrete deck surrounded the pool. The sun reflected off the clear water and showed the blue liner underneath. He'd appreciated this space the most out of any spot in the house since they bought it.

"I am hungry," Rachel proclaimed and grabbed her dress.

"You said you'd swim," Archer argued.

"Meh, later," she told him, trying to turn her dress right side out.

"You asked for it."

"Asked for what?"

She barely got the words out before Archer had his arms around her, carrying her to the pool. She held onto him for dear life, while yelling for him to put her down. Threats were made, as Archer just laughed.

She wiggled and tried to get out of his grip, while also holding on. At the edge of the pool, she just stared back at him. He knew without a doubt she was thinking that if she went down then he was coming too. Joke was on her, though, as that had been his plan.

Without another thought, Archer jumped into the six-foot section of the pool with Rachel still clinging to him. She held tighter as she sucked in a breath at the cool water surrounding them.

"You'll pay for this." She released him and tried to pull away.

"Unlikely." He pulled her back to him and dunked her head underwater.

She came up gasping for air and pushed herself away from him. Archer couldn't help but laugh as she stuck her tongue out at him before swimming further away.

Austin laughed and, with a running start, jumped in the pool with them. Archer was so stunned he barely managed to close his own gaping mouth as Austin dunked him under.

"Told you!" Rachel yelled from a safe distance across the pool and stuck her tongue out at Archer as shook the water off his face.

"It's on now," Archer dove under the water, going to Austin's legs, just missing him, he came back up for air.

"That suit was a bold choice," Archer heard Victoria say from behind him.

Victoria wasn't supposed to be here tonight, and Austin looked just as concerned as Archer felt. Rachel walked to the stairs and out of the pool, quickly pulling on her dress.

Austin quickly lifted himself out the side of the pool and looked back and forth between Victoria and Rachel, before making his way around the pool to Victoria. Archer debated if it was better to stay in the pool for only a moment.

With a sigh, he watched as Austin gave Victoria a look, and climbed out of the pool himself. Leaving Rachel at the table by herself, he stormed toward Archer and Victoria, never taking his eyes off her.

"Why would you say that to her?" Austin demanded through gritted teeth, trying to keep his voice down.

"What? I was being nice; it was a compliment," Victoria assured him.

Austin didn't look like he bought it and just left her standing there, returning to the table where Rachel was seated.

"Evening, Archer. I assume tonight's food choice was your idea?" she asked sweetly.

"You were supposed to be at some soiree tonight," he reminded her.

"Something came up." She shrugged and headed for Austin, who was deep in conversation with Rachel. "Austin, can you help me find something for me to eat?" she purred as she approached him.

"Yeah, let's go inside." He took her hand and led her into the house.

"I'm heading home," Rachel said quietly, not looking up at him.

"She wasn't supposed to be here," he told her. "We can still have a good time; please stay." He really didn't want her to leave. He'd been having fun and was pretty sure she was too.

"I'm not going to stay where I have someone making comments like that." She still didn't look at him; instead, she was carefully taking the brownies off the tray she brought and placing them next to the steaks.

"She commented on your swimsuit. So what?" He didn't understand the big deal.

"You don't get it." She looked up at him, and he could see she was fighting back tears. "It's okay that you don't get it. I'm not mad at you." She brought her left hand up and placed it on his check, giving him a sad smile. "Thank you for the invitation."

He didn't say anything as she picked up her tray. He wanted to say something, but he didn't know how to fix it or what to do. Picking up a brownie, he dropped into a chair and took a bite.

"Your brother is a real jerk sometimes," Victoria said as she came outside. "Where did Rachel go?"

"She went home."

"Just as well." Victoria looked at the food on the table. "Did she bring these?" She pointed at the brownies.

"She did; they're really good. Try one," he offered, not looking up at her, still trying to puzzle out what was going on.

"Explains a lot," he heard her say under her breath.

"What?" he asked, looking up.

"She's good at cooking sweets." Victoria smiled back at him.

"Where's Austin?"

"He went to get me something to eat that wasn't so..." She left off, just motioning to the food on the table.

"You know there's more to life than dieting, and the food is a lot better."

"So I've been told."

They chatted about nonsense for the next short while as they waited for Austin to come back. Archer made a plate for himself but didn't eat, just moving the food around. He checked his phone a few times, hoping that Rachel would text him, but didn't get any messages.

Victoria apparently was annoyed with him not paying any attention to her and had moved to the chair next to his. She reached out and placed her hand on his shoulder.

"Are you okay?" she asked, concerned.

"I'm just trying to figure some things out." He looked over at her, surprised she was so close, chairs touching, and he hadn't noticed.

"I'm so sorry. She'll come to realize what's important." Victoria rested her head on Archer's shoulder, something that she'd never done before.

Startled, he froze. She took her hand and gently trailed it up and down his forearm, causing goose bumps.

"What—What are you doing?" he sputtered, confused.

"I just want you to know that I care about you, and I understand your concern," she whispered.

Flustered at the fact that he was slowly getting turned on by his brother's girlfriend, he jumped out of his seat. She nearly fell over, he moved so quickly away from her.

"I—I gotta go."

He knocked over a chair in his haste to get away from her, putting as much distance as he could between them as quickly as possible. He needed a drink, and to forget that ever happened.

Grabbing his keys, he didn't bother changing, just ran out the door and straight to his car. He was at his studio in less than ten minutes, strong drink in his hand. He couldn't work on anything, couldn't focus, instead he sat on the floor, phone in one hand and drink in the other.

He didn't know how long he sat there. Long enough to be wobbly when he stood. Looking down at his phone, he unlocked it and opened the app for a ride to pick him up. He knew he couldn't drive anywhere, but he needed to do something.

His first instinct was to go to Rachel's. If anyone would understand his feelings, it was her. How could he have feelings for his brother's girlfriend? What was wrong with him?

Those thoughts swirled through his head the whole way to her house. The driver looked nervous as he climbed out of the car, but didn't say anything. He slipped him a twenty-dollar tip and headed for Rachel's front door.

"What are you doing here? Where is your car?" Rachel yanked the door open before he could knock. "You're drunk!"

"A little," he admitted, proud when it didn't slur. "I need to talk to you."

"You could have called." It was true. He could have done that, but it's not like he was thinking anything through right now.

She stepped in and gestured for him to come inside, shaking her head. He went straight for her living room, stretching out on the sofa like he was at a shrink's in the movies.

"Are you serious right now? What was so important that you couldn't call?"

He looked up her with her hands on her hips. She was glaring at him, but keeping her anger in check. He could see it was there; he knew her well enough to read her body language, and she was tense.

"I think I have feelings for Victoria," he said, pinching the bridge of his nose and looking up at the ceiling. It sounded worse when he said it out loud.

"Excuse me?" Rachel yelled.

"She gets me, doesn't get frustrated with me when I struggle with a menu when we all go out. She is always nice to me, and tonight she put her head on my shoulder and was rubbing my arm and I got turned on. I'm a shit brother." He dropped his arm to the sofa and sighed.

"I don't have words right now. At this rate, I need my own drink." Rachel stormed off, leaving him in the living room by himself.

He thought she'd come back. He heard her open and close a few cabinets, but she didn't come back. Slowly he brought himself to a seat before attempting to stand without the room tilting. Holding onto the walls for support, he went in search of Rachel.

"You left?" he asked.

"I can't deal with that mess. I'm going to say it once, and you can either choose to believe me or never bring her up again, but she is manipulating you both, with her pouts and sickeningly sweet fake attitude. Austin even sees it sometimes. I, for one, won't be dragged into her shit as she forces you two apart."

Rachel was sitting at her table eating the pasta she

hadn't eaten the night before when he'd been there. She cut her eyes to him now and then, but wouldn't give him her full attention.

He didn't understand why she thought that Victoria was like that. He'd never seen any of it. There were times, like tonight, where he could see how her comments could be taken wrong, but that's all it was, he was sure of it.

"You're wrong," he told her.

"No!" Rachel slammed her hands on the table as she stood. "You're wrong. Let me explain something to you. Everything she does for you, I do for you. I get no credit for that. I don't need it, but I'm not going to sit here and listen to you rave about that bitch while I listen, nope."

"You're my friend!" he yelled back at her.

"Dammit, Archer!" She stormed over to him. "I'm your best friend, but I'd be more if only you'd see it." She spoke softer as she approached him.

He heard her whisper, "Screw it," as though to herself, and then she went up on tiptoe and kissed him. His body instantly came alive. It was more than goose bumps as he put his arms around her, lifting her to the counter and deepening the kiss.

His body didn't care that this was his best friend; it only reacted to the kiss, to the woman in his arms. She moaned, gripping him to her with her legs as her hands ran through his hair and down his body.

She broke the kiss. "Archer?" She breathed his name as a question.

He opened his eyes and looked down at her. He was kissing his best friend, considering doing more, on her kitchen counter. All this after lusting after his brother's girlfriend. What was wrong with him? He shook his head and stepped back.

"I can't," he said, and with more stability than he thought he had in him, he turned and walked out her front door.

There was no plan. He just walked. Still in just his swim trunks and sandals, long since dried. No shirt, phone and keys in his pocket. He was a terrible friend, even if she meant what he said. He never should have kissed her back.

He scolded himself as he walked and attempted to sort through his thoughts. He didn't notice when a car stopped beside him, didn't hear the car door.

"Archer," he heard Austin yell, "get in the car."

He dropped his shoulders and turned around. Nodding, he let out a sigh and climbed in his brother's car.

4

———————

*T*oday was crap. Rachel had decided that before she'd even gotten out of bed this morning. She was late for work, her head was killing her, and she was exhausted.

She called Austin after Archer left her house last night and just told him that Archer was drunk and wandering around on foot. He'd left to go find him and called when he'd had him safe at home to let her know. She hadn't heard from Archer today, didn't think she would.

Mondays were rough no matter what in real estate, as there were so many calls to catch up with from places being closed over the weekend. She had new clients to take to view houses today, and it had been a miracle she'd managed to get herself presentable.

Thankfully they were easy clients and weren't like the ones the other day that had been adamant everything was just a little off in every house they'd seen. She was still scheduling more viewings for them, but these clients were calm, asked a few questions, but did a lot of their talking between themselves.

After showing them four houses, they hadn't decided and would likely call her tonight. If she was a betting person, she'd say they were going to put an offer in on the first house they saw. They were sweet and wanting to start a family; she thought it was the best one for them.

She was just pulling back into the office to run down some paperwork and return calls when her phone rang. She glanced down at it and had to look twice to be sure it was who she thought. Archer, was calling her and it was barely lunch. Rejecting the call, she got out of her car and went inside. She wasn't ready to face last night's humiliation just yet.

"Hey, Rachel, you have messages on your desk and few voicemails," Jane, the office receptionist and her best girl-friend, said as she walked in.

"Thanks," she mumbled, heading for her office.

"Are you okay?" Jane followed her.

"Shut the door?" Rachel said as she set her bag down.

"Oh no, what happened?" Jane sounded concerned as she quietly closed the door behind her, taking a seat.

"I kissed Archer last night." Rachel sat in her own chair and rested her head in her hands on the desk.

"What?" Jane let out a squeal.

"Shh," she told her. If she kept that up, the whole office was going to join them.

"So, what was it like?" she whispered.

Rachel took a steadying breath before answering her. "It was great. It was everything I imagined." She looked at Jane's excited face, watching it fall with her next words. "Right up until he walked away, right out my front door, and never looked back."

Just saying it out loud made her want to start crying all over again. She never should have kissed him, and definitely not last night when he was drunk and already on edge with Victoria on his mind.

"I'm so sorry. Want me to go fight him?" Jane offered.

She couldn't help but laugh. Jane was five foot tall and had never fought anything in her life. They'd known each other as long as the Stone twins, and had always been close.

"Thank you, but I think I'll manage. I appreciate it though." She held up her phone for Jane to see. "He called as I was pulling up. I didn't answer."

"Maybe he changed his mind?"

"He was drunk, Jane. I overstepped. This is on me, and I don't want to face it yet."

"I'm sorry. Let me know how I can help?"

"I will. Thank you." She got up as Jane did, and gave her a hug. "I mean it. Thank you."

"We can do something this weekend?" Jane offered.

"Yes please!" She needed to do something, probably before the weekend if she were honest.

Jane shut her office door on the way out, and Rachel leaned back in her chair, letting out a breath. Today was just crap, and she was done. Her phone rang again, and she considered not even looking at it.

She reached forward and picked it up off the desk, seeing Archer's name on the screen again. With a resigned sigh, she sat up and answered the call.

"Hello?" she answered timidly, unsure of where this was headed and already feeling her face turn red with embarrassment over last night.

"Hey! I was starting to think you were avoiding me," Archer teased.

I was, she thought. "Just busy Monday stuff. What's up?"

"I figured I probably owe you dinner after last night. Thought I could cook it at your place tonight?"

"What? Why? Why would you think that?" She leaned forward and rested her elbow on her desk and her head in her hand.

"Well, you left without eating last night." He said like it was obvious.

She had left without eating, but what did that mean? Did he not remember what happened last night? The pit that was already in her stomach got heavier at the thought.

"Umm, maybe not. It's been a rough day today. Another time." She didn't want to hang out with him so soon after last night, especially while she tried to cope with him not acknowledging last night.

"Come on, Rach. I feel bad. Plus, I didn't eat either."

"Arch, I don't know."

"Come on, you're going to eat anyway. Just have some company, and you won't have to cook, or eat that stupid fake pasta."

"The stupid fake pasta is good for you!" she defended, but it *was* stupid fake pasta, and she didn't care for it.

"Please?" he asked.

"Ugh. Fine," she relented while kicking herself for it.

"Awesome! I'll see you tonight."

He ended the call, and she stared at the phone. What had she done? Now she was going to have to face him tonight? What if he was just waiting to talk to her about it in person? She was going to be sick for certain.

She sent a message to Jane and asked her to come here if she was free. Knowing Jane, she'd be here even if she wasn't; there was likely going to be a call on hold somewhere.

"What's up?" Jane whispered as she came in and shut the door. "Did he call again?"

"Yes." She pouted. "And he's coming over to cook dinner tonight."

"What? That's great news."

"He didn't mention what happened. I don't know what that means."

"Maybe he wants to kiss you again." Jane smiled.

"I don't think so. Ugh, what do I do?" she asked.

"Go home and shower and get ready for some sexy time?" Jane kept the smile on her face.

"What if he wants to let me down in person?" she worried.

"Then you need to get on a dating app and still have sexy time." Like it was that easy.

"I am not that kind of person," she told Jane with a glare.

"You should try it sometime. I'm not near as pent up as you are." Jane stood, opening the door. "Suit yourself though, but I think a mental health day wouldn't be frowned on."

Jane slipped out the door before Rachel could reply. She wasn't wrong on the day off. It wasn't like she was getting anything done anyway. She grabbed her bag, deciding home was better than here for the overthinking she was doing already.

"Take messages?" she asked Jane as she walked past.

"Call me later?" Jane asked instead of answering.

"Of course."

5

———

Archer showed up to Rachel's that evening with groceries in hand. He didn't know how things were going to go tonight, but he did want to try to make things up to her. He remembered everything from last night, but he knew he didn't handle it well at all and still wasn't sure how to handle it.

He didn't have feelings for Rachel as anything other than a friend, but he didn't want to hurt her feelings. More than that, he didn't want to lose their friendship. For now, he was going to pretend like nothing happened and hope everything would be the same.

There was no plan tonight. He just wanted to have a good time with his friend. Yesterday had been terrible for him, and he assumed for her as well. He still didn't fully understand her issues with Victoria, but that didn't mean he didn't understand that she was upset.

Rachel opened the door for him as he walked up, something she always did whenever she knew he was coming. Smiling, he held up the bag of groceries as he walked in.

"What all is in there?" She closed the door and followed him to the kitchen.

"A little bit of everything." He started pulling out potatoes.

She walked to the other side of him and grabbed at the bag.

"Nope. Go sit. I'm cooking." He pushed her away with his hip.

"Really?" She rolled her eyes at him.

"Really, now go."

"Whatever. I have work to do anyway."

She disappeared for a bit as Archer prepped things for dinner. He knew his way around her kitchen better than his own. Everything was in a spot that made the most amount of sense, way better than the decorator had done with his kitchen, which was for aesthetic.

Opening the back door, he stepped out onto her deck and pulled the cover off the grill. He was fairly positive that no one used this except him, certainly not the owner herself. No doubt something she'd bought for him that he kept at her house.

That thought made him pause. How much else was here that was bought or set up with him in mind? He'd never thought about it, but there were little bits of him throughout her house. He even had clothes and toiletries in her spare room.

Frozen halfway to opening the grill, he wondered what else he hadn't paid attention to, and why he was now. Well, that's not true; he knew why now. It was the kiss and what she'd told him last night.

He hadn't quite wrapped his head around it, her telling him she liked him in that way. It wasn't any less weird than him suddenly lusting after Victoria, but somehow it also was.

She never came out as he cooked the steaks. He came back in with them to let them rest while he fixed the mac and cheese they'd missed out on last night. It was probably why he'd gotten as drunk as he did last night: he hadn't eaten anything.

Rachel was sitting at the table on her computer, glass of wine in her hand and her glasses on. She rarely wore them, usually it was contacts, but when she was home and done for the day, she'd switch them out.

Stirring the pasta, he looked over at her. Legs up in the chair, he knew she was comfortable. Her hair was wet, down, and slightly dripping, a darker brown when it was wet. She had on comfortable shorts that he knew had a hole in them.

She didn't look up at him or speak, as he continued to watch. He had to admit, it was a really domestic thing, her sitting there working as he cooked them a meal, the silence not awkward. It was something he'd imagined having with his future girlfriend, just comfortable.

Looking away, he grabbed the colander and strained the pasta, his thoughts more confused than ever. If he wanted this with someone else, how was it different with Rachel? That was something he needed to work out and see what it was Rachel was seeing, because he was starting to wonder if he did see her differently now that he was thinking about it.

"You going to dress those noodles?" She pulled him from his thoughts.

"Oh." He quickly grabbed the packet of liquid cheese-like product. "Doing that now. You ready to eat?"

"I'm hungry for sure."

Rachel returned to her computer, and he listened to her tap away. By the time he had plated the food, she was closing the laptop and putting it to the side.

"What happened at work today?" he asked as he carried the food to the table.

"Huh?" She drew her brows together in confusion as she looked up at him.

"You said it was a rough day?"

"Oh, I didn't realize I'd said that. It was just a typical Monday, and I've had a touch of a headache all day." To emphasize that, she rubbed her forehead.

"That sucks."

They ate in silence, and he kept hoping she would pick the conversation back up as she normally would have, but she didn't. In fact, she barely looked at him, only focusing on her plate.

He continued to study her and look around her kitchen as he ate. The more he sat there, the more he wondered if he had things all wrong with Rachel. Maybe it was more than friendship, but, if they were wrong, there was no more friendship.

"I'll clean up so you can finish working, and get out of your way." Now that he'd let all these thoughts in, he needed to go sort through them.

"I can clean up. Thanks for dinner."

He wanted to argue with her, but the look on her face said she wanted him to leave. She seemed nervous, and he wasn't helping, watching her like he was.

"Thanks for letting me try to make it up to you."

She gave him a sad smile, the only kind of smile he'd gotten from her today. "Yep. I've got a lot to do, so I'll see you later."

He nodded, picking up his plate and putting it in the sink. "Guess I'll leave you to it then."

He awkwardly stood there for another minute before giving a slight wave and leaving. As he walked to his car, he turned and looked at her house, somewhere he lived half the time, and wondered what it all meant.

6

___

*A*rcher was on her nerves more than usual lately. In the past week he'd been at her house almost every day. That wasn't odd, although she did long for a break after her rushed confession last week.

No, it was the fact that he was constantly watching her. It was so hard to get work done with someone staring at you. She'd tried hard not to acknowledge him, but it was getting more and more uncomfortable.

She still wondered if he was lying about not remembering anything else from Sunday night, but it would have been unlike him to not say anything. He was a talk-it-out person when it came to her, and she expected that if he did remember that he would be talking to her about it, or even avoiding her.

"What?" she finally broke and asked.

"Huh?" he answered, as though she hadn't looked up right into his eyes as they stared at her.

"You're watching me. What do you want?"

"I'm not watching you," he lied.

"Seriously, I don't know if I have a giant zit on my forehead or what, but stop. It's weird," she scolded him.

"You don't have a zit that I see." He grinned.

"I'm not kidding. I don't know what you're doing, but stop."

"Whatever."

She rolled her eyes and stuck her tongue out at him as he finally turned away from her. It was weirding her out, and that was being nice.

With a resigned sigh, she decided to approach the topic again to see if she could find out what was going on. "What's on your mind?"

"Not much, why?" he asked, not looking back at her again.

They were in her living room, and it was already late, even for a Friday night. He was in her recliner, and she was stretched out on the couch, sitting with her legs taking up two cushions. They were supposed to be relaxing and watching a movie, but it wasn't going well so far.

"You seem lost in your thoughts all week. What is it?" She wasn't even sure she wanted to know at this point.

"Nothing. I've just been thinking about what to do next."

"Next? With what?" she probed further. Apparently he was going to make her fight for each piece of information.

"With my art," he explained. "I've been offered a pretty sizable commission. Not sure if I want to do it."

That wasn't it, she decided immediately. He was still looking at the TV instead of her, but she'd go along with it anyway.

"What's the issue?"

"I'm not sure I'm feeling it." He finally looked back at her. "I don't want to talk about it right now," he told her.

"Okay. Let me know if you do, or if you need help with anything."

Years ago, she'd helped him and read almost anything out loud for him to help him sort through it without adding his dyslexia into it. Now, there were screen readers, talk to text, and a million other ways that he could help himself. He'd also finally gotten with a great teacher, though really late in high school, who gave him a lot of tips.

However, the only thing she believed from him tonight was that he didn't want to talk about whatever was bothering him. She wanted to ask Austin, but with Victoria always around him, she didn't call. She'd lose her mind if she caught them talking, jealous brat.

He could have been obsessing over Victoria now instead. She really thought he was being manipulated, but he didn't want to hear it. For some reason, he believed her every time instead of Rachel.

That grated on her nerves more than the person herself. Victoria was always seen as the saint to him, making him question Rachel constantly. And the sickeningly sweet way that she delivered her insults made it look like Rachel was overreacting.

Austin, to his credit, had recently started to see Victoria's insults for what they were. She didn't know what was going on in their relationship, of course, but she secretly hoped it meant that she might not be around too much longer.

She also hated that the insults got to her the way that they did. The swimsuit comment from last weekend had really bothered her. More so because she knew she had gained a few pounds, but she didn't think it looked terrible in that swimsuit. Apparently, the extra pounds were more noticeable than she thought.

"I am going to get ready for bed. It's late." She decided it was better to overthink this from the bed in hope of sleep instead of out here with him.

"Oh, okay. I think I'll stay and finish watching the movie."

"Umm..." She paused; she'd been kind of hoping he would leave. "I guess that's okay. Good night."

She grabbed her glass and put it in the sink, leaving him in the kitchen. It was bad enough that he forgot her confession and kiss, that he'd told her he wasn't interested, but now he had invaded more of her life than normal, and she was struggling to figure it all out.

It wasn't like she was able to just turn her feelings off either. She still wanted him, even though she knew he didn't want her. She still wanted him to want her, more than anything that's what she wanted.

With him being here all the time, she'd had no time to go through her own thoughts. Jane had talked with her all week, but she was more optimistic, thinking that Archer had somehow suddenly developed feelings for her and that's why he was around. It was probably at least partially due to him avoiding Victoria, but was he just going to move in at this point? And would she let him?

Tomorrow she would try to get him to leave. She needed her house back. She might even go to the pound and get a cat to keep her company instead.

Smiling, she lay back in her bed. That was a great plan. She'd always wanted a pet, and a cat didn't need her attention all the time the way a dog would. She was going to do that tomorrow as soon as she got Archer out of her house and, hopefully, out of her brain for five minutes.

7

Archer was a chicken; he knew it. He'd been hiding out at Rachel's since last weekend, avoiding both Austin and Victoria. Austin had lectured him after he'd left Rachel's drunk. He'd deserved it, but it didn't mean he was going back for more.

There was also the matter of being turned on by Victoria, which had him all types of confused. He still didn't understand how that had happened. Maybe he just needed to get laid.

He was still laying in the guest room at Rachel's. He'd heard her get up an hour ago and move around. She'd knocked on his door, but he'd pretended to be asleep. She knew something was wrong with him, but if she only knew what it was, she'd probably be even more upset.

She had texted him and told him she was going to the gym not long after she knocked. He was waiting until he was sure she was gone to get up, listening to every movement in the house, waiting to hear the front door close.

Finally, he heard her leave, and Archer got out of bed and looked around. He wasn't coming back here tonight. He was going to do literally anything else; he needed to get away from her so he could think. Unfortunately, home wasn't a viable option either.

He got dressed and threw his sheets in the washer, something he always did when he stayed over for a while, cleaning up after himself. Having grown up with maids and never doing his own laundry, it had been Rachel that had taught him that skill. She'd also pressed into him the need to clean up his own mess.

After doing that, he left, heading for his studio. He waited until he arrived to text Rachel and let her know to switch the sheets out and that he wouldn't be coming over tonight. If he hadn't hid there for a week, he wouldn't have felt the need to check in with her about not coming back.

Around lunch, he figured most of his friends would be up, and he set about making some plans. First the beach, then the club. He needed to get out, and that was exactly what he was going to do: bonus if he could find a willing woman tonight too.

Plans in place, he felt better than he had in a week. He wasn't lying to Rachel last night; he did have a commission to decide on, so he set about reviewing that once again. Of course, when she'd asked what was on his mind last night, it wasn't this. It should have been, but it was her. He wasn't going to tell her that though.

The piece would be massive, and he had creative reign over the project, but he wasn't sure he wanted to do it. He'd gotten this commission on Tuesday, and he'd had no muse, no interest in art this week. Now, he felt more free and was considering it at more length.

"Yo!" he heard Rob calling as he came into the studio.

"Sup?" he answered with a handshake.

"Surprised you wanted to hang out. Thought you forgot about us all."

Archer stepped back. It had been a while since he hung out with anyone. "Nah, man, just busy."

"Well, glad to have you. You ready?" He looked Archer up and down. "Dude, this was your idea, and you aren't even dressed for the beach?"

"Shit, lost track of time. Give me a minute; I have clothes here."

"You live here now?" Rob wandered around his studio looking at the half-finished pieces and general mess that made up the majority of it.

"No, I just lose track of time, so I keep some clothes here."

"Your girl Rachel coming today?" he asked.

Archer was pulling on his trunks and nearly fell over at the question. "What?" he yelled back.

"Rachel? Is she coming?" Rob asked again.

He left the bathroom and looked at Rob. He was bleach blond, tanned, and every bit as tall as Archer was. Rob was much more muscular, where Archer was lean. He didn't look bad with his shirt off, but Rob was constantly working out when he wasn't partying.

"Why?" Archer asked, pretty sure he didn't want to know the answer.

"She's hot, man." Rob shrugged as if the answer was obvious.

"No, she's not. Leave her alone," he cautioned.

Rob threw both hands up in defense. "Hey now, if you aren't going to tap it, you can't stop her from wanting this."

"She's not interested; trust me." He didn't have a clue if she was or not, hadn't thought about it before. Rachel usually dated men like Austin, the kind that wore suits to work and partied never.

"She was interested at the gym this morning."

Archer took several deep breaths as he searched for a pair of sandals that he knew were there somewhere. What had Rachel said at the gym this morning? Why did it matter? Pulling his sandals from under the desk, he slid them on.

"Let's go."

They spent the day at the beach, Archer, Rob, and five other men, just hanging out, playing some catch with a football someone had brought. As the sun went down, they left the beach and wandered the strip, deciding which bar they wanted to start with.

A dive that they frequented was at the end. Starting there, they decided they could make their way down the strip, something they had done may times before, pretty much since one of them was old enough to buy the alcohol.

The whole strip was crowded as they walked down. It was the height of summer, and the tourists mixed with the locals to have fun. It didn't take long for the group of guys to find a group of women to hang out with.

Archer had a blonde named Trina on his arm within minutes of stepping into the bar. Her hair was bleached, pulled back in a high ponytail, and she still wore her swimsuit with just a pair of short cutoff jean shorts, fly open, showing she was still wearing her bikini bottom as well.

He ordered them drinks and took a seat at the table, pulling her onto his lap. They flirted as the music played, and Archer lost track of his friends' conversation.

At the next bar, and several shots later, Archer still had Trina on his lap. It was getting later, and he was ready to get out of there soon, hopefully with her.

"Are you from around here?" he yelled over the music.

"No, New York," she answered.

"You staying nearby?" he asked, preparing to clear his mind tonight of both women that had been plaguing him.

"Walking distance." She winked at him and giggled.

Archer threw back the rest of his beer. "Need another?" he asked her, gesturing to her fruity cocktail.

"Please!" She stirred it around with the straw before closing her lips around it and taking a big sip.

He adjusted himself in the chair so she could feel his cock straining underneath her. He cupped the back of her neck with his hand and brought her lips to his for a deep kiss before she stood so he could get more drinks.

"Hey, man." Rob came up, tapping him on the back. "She's hot."

"Just what I needed tonight," Archer told him.

"Rachel and Jane are on their way down if you want to head out before she gives you a hard time."

Archer slowly turned to look at his friend, considering his next words. "How would you know?"

"I invited her down. She said yeah and was picking up Jane on the way."

"What the hell? I told you to leave her alone!" They were already yelling to talk over the music, but Archer was louder than all of it now.

"You're not her keeper, man. She's grown." Rob folded his arms across his chest, daring Archer to say something.

"I. Told. You. Leave. Her. Alone." Each word was enhanced with a full stop through gritted teeth.

"So, she can't get laid because she's friends with you? What the hell, man? Where'd all this come from?" Rob kept his arms crossed, his fingers holding the bottle of beer by the top, swaying it back and forth against his side.

"None of your damn business. She's too good for the lot of us and doesn't need to come down here and get mixed up in your shit."

"My shit?" He unfolded his arms and took a long swig of his beer. "This whole night was your fucking idea!"

"It didn't include her!" Archer roared, shoving Rob as he did.

Unprepared, Rob fell backward onto the ground, his beer spilling next to him. The entire bar turned to look at them as Rob scrambled back to his feet.

"What is wrong with you?"

Rob shoved him back, but Archer was ready and didn't so much as flinch. Having embarrassed him, he knew what was coming and was ready for the swing when Rob took it, dodging it with ease.

8

The fight had ended with the police being called and both of them getting arrested. He'd been arrested before, so had Rob, but never for fighting each other. They slept it off and were able to leave the next morning.

He'd called the only person he could think of that wasn't his brother: Rachel. She came, of course, and he will never forget the look of disappointment that she gave him as he climbed in her car. The ride back to her house had been silent, a trend that had lasted two days.

It wasn't until tonight that she finally started a conversation with him, and now he wished she hadn't. He preferred silence to the reminder that he needed to go home and deal with his mess.

"I'm not going home yet," he told her.

"You need to talk to your brother." Her voice was calm, like she was talking to a stubborn child, and that pissed him off more.

"If you don't want me here, I can stay somewhere else," he offered.

"That's not what I said." She stood in the kitchen as they sorted takeout boxes, "You're just avoiding the inevitable."

"Maybe I am, and I'm going to continue to do that."

"You can't avoid it forever," she warned.

"I can't, but I can avoid it right now."

"Have you at least answered their calls?" She put her hand on her hip as she waited for him to answer.

"My phone isn't even on." He wasn't ignoring anyone if he didn't know they called.

She shook her head. "I thought you were better than that." It was said very softly, but he understood each and every word, and the disappointment that she'd had in him for the last few days laced between them.

"I thought you were my friend?" he threw out.

Her mouth fell open before she quickly recovered. "How dare you! Are you not staying here, in my house, while you hide from the problems you started? Did I not pick you up from jail?" She threw the plastic fork she'd only just picked up down onto her plate.

"What do you mean that I started? I didn't start that; Rob did." He might have gotten physical first, but Rob had started it by inviting Rachel.

"That's not what I heard, and I was there right after y'all were arrested."

"Whatever" was his lame answer.

"What the hell is going on with you?" She picked her fork back up and carried the plate, she'd been standing at the counter eating from, out of the kitchen, away from him.

It seemed no matter what he did, he was in the wrong and pissing everyone off. He needed to get things back to some sort of normal again. If only he knew how.

He grabbed his own plate and followed her to the living room. She didn't speak as he sat next to her on the couch.

Hell, he hadn't known until right then that she was capable of eating angrily.

"Look, I didn't start it, not really. Rob said some things before it started," he offered.

"I have no doubt. But what matters is how you handle it." She took a bite and swallowed before continuing. "You have to own up to the fact that you messed up, no matter the reason."

She was right, he had to admit, but stopped short of being able to admit it out loud. If he continued on this topic, she was going to ask what Rob said, and there was no chance he was going there. At this point he just hoped Rob kept his mouth shut.

"Look." She set her fork down again and turned toward him, shifting her hips to face him. "I'm not trying to tell you what to do..."

Archer raised an eyebrow at her. Wasn't that exactly what she was doing?

"Okay, maybe I am. But you have to own up to it, Archer. You can stay here as long as you need to, but you know eventually you will have to own this mess."

"I know I will have to eventually." He ran his hand through his hair, taking a deep breath. "But not today, okay?"

"Okay."

She gave in and went back to her plate. He knew the conversation wasn't really over, it was only paused for now, but he'd take it. He picked his plate up, eating the food but not tasting it, as he tried to figure out the best way to deal with all of it.

Rachel's phone rang, and she picked it up, motioning to him that she'd be right back. He didn't watch as she left, figuring it was likely work and she'd be back when she was done.

He'd go home tomorrow and talk to Austin. Hopefully his parents weren't aware of what happened, but that was unlikely. He didn't even want to turn his phone on, didn't want to know all the angry messages he'd have waiting for him. Instead, he'd talk to Austin first and then deal with each thing as it came.

Rachel was taking a long time, he thought as he finished his own plate. He leaned back on the couch and started flipping channels, looking for something to pass the time tonight.

"What the hell?" Rachel stormed into the living room.

"What?" He jumped forward, wondering what was wrong.

She leveled him with a glare that rivaled any school teacher he'd ever seen. Archer froze.

"What was the fight about?"

"Wait, what?" he asked, dumbfounded at the direction this conversation had gone.

"The fight with Rob, what was it about?" She was shaking, her face was red, as she stared him down.

He hesitated to answer. Wondering who she had just spoken to and where this had come from. "Why?" he ventured.

"Why not?" she countered.

When he didn't respond, she started pacing. She would turn and look at him, opening her mouth to say something and then start pacing again.

"Did you get into a fight with Rob because he invited me?" she asked, her voice too calm.

"Who did you talk to?" He stood, getting angry that someone would call to tell her that.

"What does that matter? Was that the reason for the fight?" she shouted, stopping her pacing to stare at him.

Archer stood now too, feeling himself growing restless. "It wasn't like that" was all he said.

"So, I'm good enough to hang out with here, and you can crash at my house for an indefinite amount of time, but I'm not good enough to hang out with at the bar or anywhere else?" She grew more animated as she spoke, her hands moving with each word.

"That wasn't it at all!" he yelled at her.

Of all the things she might have taken from that fight, this threw him for a loop. He never thought she'd take it this way, as though it was an offense to her. If anything, it was an offense to Rob, hell, to himself, but never her.

"Funny, because it damn sure seems like it." She picked up her plate off the coffee table and looked at him again. "I'm going to my room. I expect you to find somewhere else to stay before I get home from work tomorrow."

She started to walk away, and Archer reached out for her arm.

"Don't touch me," she said angrily, yanking her arm away from him.

"Just listen to me, please?"

"I don't think you have anything to say that I want to hear." She walked away.

He followed her, trying his best to explain. "I didn't want you out with him. I told him earlier that day that you were off-limits, and he still invited you out!" He had no sooner said it than he wished he could take it back.

"Off-limits? Who are you to decide?" Fury radiated off her, and Archer took a step back.

"He just wants to get in your pants!" Archer snapped.

"And? Who are you to decide if I want to let him or not? It's not now and has never been your place."

Archer stared her down. "You're too good for him and that bullshit."

"Yeah, right, why don't you just say what it is?"

He stared at her, confused as to where this was going.

"You don't want me, but you need me to be here for you, so you always have a place to hide. You want me to continue on as we always have and never mix with your real friends so long as you need me."

Rachel made to walk away, and he did the only thing he could think of, pulling her to him in a deep kiss. He hadn't intended it, but the moment his lips touched hers, he never wanted to let her go.

She leaned into the kiss, holding him tightly to her, before she suddenly pulled away. "Don't do this. Don't tease me to get what you want from me."

"Rach, I swear to you I have never been more serious than I am right at this moment." He looked her in her eyes, pouring all he had into those words.

9

———

*R*achel was stunned. Completely and utterly shook to her core. Archer wanted her, right now, and she was going to simply pass out from the excitement.

She took a deep breath. "Are you positive?"

"Don't question me on this again. I know what I want," Archer told her.

To her never-ending surprise, Archer picked her up, holding her against him. Her legs straddled him as her arms held tightly to his neck.

He kissed her as his hands held her ass. They were moving, and she turned to see where they were going, her room it appeared, as he laid her down on the bed.

"Archer...," she started.

"I swear to God if you ask me if I'm sure one more time, I'm going to leave you here."

She giggled, "I was just going to say I don't have any protection."

"On it." He ran out of her room and across the hall to his own, returning with a condom.

She wanted to ask why he had that and who it had been

intended for, but bit her lip instead. It definitely wasn't in her best interest to be having those thoughts right now.

Archer laid over her, both their legs still off the side of the bed. "Now, where were we?" He kissed her lips. "This seems about right."

Rachel couldn't help it, she giggled. Raising her arms, she ran her hands through his hair and pressed her lips back to his. His tongue searched, and she opened her lips, matching his eager passion.

She was stuck in a trance somewhere between I can't believe this is happening and this is really happening. At anytime now she was going to wake up from this dream in a sweat and be sad that it was only a dream, she was sure of it.

"Rachel," Archer stared down at her, "are you sure?"

She nodded her response, afraid to speak.

"Then stop thinking so much."

She nodded again and attempted to clear her mind, not an easy thing for her to do in any situation.

"Let me help," Archer offered and took her mouth in another kiss.

This kiss was different, better, deeper, just more. The passion and desire that they both poured into it took her breath away and she was helpless to stop it.

Archer pulled back and chuckled at her whine from the loss of his lips on hers. He tore his shirt over his head and tossed it on the ground.

She raised up and tossed her own shirt, no bra to take care of, she shimmied out of her shorts and panties, watching Archer's gaze as she did. He gaze touched every inch of her skin and she shivered in excitement.

He pulled his own pants off, boxers at the same time and picked the condom up off the bed. "Lay back," he demanded as he laid over her.

His cock lay right at her entrance and writhed beneath him, seeking more of him.

"Slowly," he whispered.

And slowly he did, little by little he filled her. He was painfully slow and it was amazingly pleasurable. He filled her and slowly slid back out before repeating the process.

"More," she begged as he continued to torment her.

He drew out one more time and positioned her hips so they were tilted upwards before thrusting in and filling her completely in well swift thrust. She cried out and grabbed the blankets in tight fists to hold on as he built a rhythm and her body sang with pleasure.

The white hot burning bead of pleasure built quickly before pushing her over the edge. She released in a fog of excitement as Archer continued to seek his pleasure.

She felt him still as he cried out and clenched her hips as he found his own peak. He held her there for a beat as they both attempted to catch their breath and slow their beating hearts.

He slowly slid from her and backed off the bed before leaving the room. In a panic she nearly cried out for him to come back, but turned in the bed instead, pulling the covers over her.

Archer returned moments later and pulled her to him, their bodies both still damp from their lovemaking. He curled one arm around her, holding her tight to him before relaxing.

She smiled as she laid there, feeling his breath on her neck and his arm around her waist. This was heaven.

10

He couldn't help it, but he'd been grateful when Rachel had to work the next morning. The sex had been better than amazing, there wasn't even a word for it, but how did one act when you slept with your best friend last night? He sure as hell didn't know.

The mess he was creating for himself was only getting bigger. Instead of sticking around until she got home, Archer got dressed and headed home. Austin was unlikely to be there yet, but he planned to be there when he did get home.

The ride back to his house, he left the radio off and rolled the windows down. He was exhausted and didn't even remember the drive. It was like he had completely blanked out; he was on muscle memory the whole way home.

Austin was sitting in the living room when he walked in.

"Hey," Archer said, seeing him there.

"Don't." Austin stood. "Don't walk in here like nothing happened and nothing is wrong."

"I wasn't." Archer meant it. He knew he had to own up to

his mistakes, and he had missed his brother, lectures and all.

"You just hid at Rachel's like I wouldn't be worried about you or want to hear from you?" Austin had always been like Archer's parent, the only one that really gave a crap about him in the family. "Plus, I have to keep fielding calls from Dad, like that's drama I need on my plate right now."

Archer waited and listened as Austin talked. He knew Austin just needed to get it all out and he'd lose steam. Any time that Archer had majorly messed up, he'd always had him there to let him know, but he knew it came from a place of caring. Unlike when he had to listen to his father scream at him and then finally dismiss him.

"Well?" Austin asked.

Archer had been lost in his own thoughts and had missed what Austin had asked. He struggled to find an answer to a question he didn't know. Instead, he went with what he really needed to talk to his brother about.

"I slept with Rachel."

"*What?*" His brother's face turned red as he yelled, incredulously. "How could you?"

"I don't know what to do now." Archer dropped himself onto one of the dark brown leather armchairs. "What if I messed everything up?"

Austin stared at him confused, before blowing out a breath with the rest of his anger, and dropping onto the opposite chair. "Why?"

He explained what happened the weekend that Austin had to pick him up and what had happened between him and Rachel that night. He left out the part about Victoria, of course.

"Shit" was his brother's only reaction as he leaned

forward in the chair, resting his arms on his knees. "Well, that explains the fight, I guess. Are you two a couple now?"

"I don't know. I don't know what to do from here," Archer confessed. Screw everything else going on, what was he supposed to do now?

"Well, hate to break it to you, but I'm not sure I can help with this," Austin told him.

"I just needed to talk about it." It was true, he wasn't expecting answers, but it felt good to get it all off his chest and to talk to someone about it.

"She's our friend…" It seemed Austin was having as much trouble processing recent events as he was. "What did she say this morning?"

"I… umm… haven't talked to her today," he answered guiltily.

"Tell me you didn't sneak out?"

"Of course not! She had to work, and I left after her."

"But your phone is off? Did you leave her a note or anything?"

"Well, no." He didn't think to leave a note for her. He'd never had to do anything like that before.

"Turn your phone on!" Austin jumped up.

"Fine."

In seconds his phone was going crazy. All the messages from the last few days, voicemails, emails, all coming through at once. He set it in the table and left Austin and the phone in the living room.

"Where are you going?" Austin called after him.

"To get something to eat. My phone is going to do that for a while." He shrugged. There was nothing he could do right now with his phone.

With food in hand and his phone no longer lighting up

nonstop, he finally picked it up. There were a ton of messages from Austin, which he didn't need to read right now, but only one from Rachel: a simple "Good morning."

He opened it to reply just as Austin and Victoria walked in. He gave Austin a knowing look to ask if he had told Victoria about Rachel. Austin shook his head in response.

"Hi, Archer. Heard you got in some trouble," Victoria said by way of greeting.

"You could say that," he replied casually. Turning off his phone, he slipped it into his pocket and sat back in the chair.

"I bet. Heard it was about Rachel. What foolishness!" She giggled and then rested her hand on Austin's shoulder.

"What's that supposed to mean?" Austin stepped away, causing her hand to fall.

"Who would fight over her?"

It wasn't her usually sweet demeanor; instead, everything finally clicked for Archer. Her voice carried a tone of derision, clearly telling them both what she really thought of Rachel.

Mentally he kicked his own butt for not noticing. He wasn't sure why the mask had slipped today, but he was grateful he'd seen a glimpse of what Rachel had always known.

"Victoria!" Austin admonished.

"What?" she said, back to her sweet tone again.

"I'm gonna head to my room, give you guys some privacy." Archer stood, making his way past the couple.

"You don't have to leave on my account." Victoria brought her left hand up and placed it on his chest as he walked past.

He looked over at her, her sweet smile annoying him

today. He thought about saying something, but instead, took a step to the right and went around her. She looked shocked as he did and he heard her huff as he left the living room.

11

———

It had been almost a full week since she and Archer had slept together, and other than a few one-word texts, she hadn't really heard from him. He had spent almost a week living with her, and now they were just nothing. She was confused—no, more than that, she was hurt.

She felt used and was over him. She hadn't texted him since Thursday, which meant that was the last time she heard from him. Saturday now, she was trying to convince herself to stop stressing it, but hadn't figured out how yet.

She tied her sneakers, grabbed her gym bag, and headed out. She'd work out and jam to the music in the gym, and hopefully her mind would focus on what she was doing instead of anything else.

It was only about a ten-minute drive to get there, and before she knew it, she was parking and getting out. The gym was always more busy on a Saturday than it was during the week, and most of the machines were already taken before she walked in.

Rob smiled as she walked in, greeting her. "Hey, girl!" he said as he walked up to her.

"Hey, yourself." Returning his smile, she walked over to the lockers, sliding in her bag and locking it.

"Wanna pair up?" he asked, as he always did.

Normally she would turn him down, but today she was in a different mood. "Actually, yes."

"Wait. For real?" His eyes were big when he turned to look at her.

"Sure, why not." She shrugged.

"What were you planning on doing this morning?"

"Definitely going for a run, but then whatever. I just need to get my mind off some things," she replied casually.

"Archer?" He was hesitant, she could tell, to ask that question, but wasn't surprised when he'd asked.

"Something like that. You running with me?" she asked, reaching the row of treadmills where there were two empty.

"Not much of a treadmill guy myself, but sure, why not?"

They ran next to each other for a while, making conversation and laughing. Rob told the worst jokes and had the funniest stories any time she talked to him.

After the third time she nearly fell from laughing, she slowed to a walk, cooling down.

"Oh, thank God." Rob tapped the button, slowing the speed on his own treadmill. "Not gonna lie, I was on the verge of quitting."

"Sure you were," she teased back, rolling her eyes. She knew him. He ran often, just normally up and down the boardwalk, not in the gym. He was here for weights. "Your turn. What's next?"

They finished their cooldown, and Rob walked her over to a weight machine, adjusting it.

"Sit here." He gestured toward the bench of the

machine. "You're going to grab these handles and pull down to your sides. Let me know if it's too much."

She wanted to be offended by his assumption that she might be weak, but he was probably right. She did some weights, but mostly free weights, using a routine she'd been taught last summer from a trainer that worked at the gym.

Grabbing both handles, she pulled too quickly and the weights jumped up and then slammed down, surprising them both.

"Okay, so not enough. Hang on."

Once he had the weights to the right setting, he turned back to her and she tried again. This time with more resistance, she didn't sling the weights as she had. He watched as she worked out, correcting her form here and there as they moved to different machines.

She was walking to her locker when she heard a phone vibrating. Quickly, she unlocked it, and grabbed her phone. Surprisingly, it was Austin reaching out to her.

"I'll call him back in a bit," she said, silencing the phone and slipping it into her bag. She didn't shower at the gym; she lived too close and found she preferred her own bathroom.

"So, do you have plans for tonight?" Rob asked.

"I don't." She knew what he was going to ask and couldn't decide if she wanted to say yes or no.

"How about a do-over of last weekend?" he offered.

Looking up at him, she smiled, still not sure how to answer that. "Maybe. Let me go shower and see how sore I am later?" It was an easy non-committal way to answer.

"Sounds good. Text me?"

She nodded and watched him as he walked to his own locker. He was built, tan, and unbelievably gorgeous, but she wasn't sure he was what she wanted. Then again, she got what she wanted earlier this week, and look how that turned out for her.

The short drive home didn't clear her mind, so she was hoping the shower would, but as she climbed out of her car, she wondered if she would have to say no, because she was sore, already feeling it. She groaned as she set her bag down and toed off her shoes.

It was amazing how good a shower could make you feel, she thought as she got dressed. Her doorbell rang as she pulled on her shorts, causing her to pause. If it was Rob, she wasn't going out with him tonight for sure. Sighing, she headed for the door.

"Austin?" That was the last person she expected. "I was going to call you back." Stepping back, she motioned for him to come in.

"I know you have a lot going on with Archer already, but—"

She cut him off, feeling her face grow hot with embarrassment, "He told you?"

"Of course he did, and he's screwing everything up right now if you ask me, but no one did."

"He is, but that's his issue, not yours," she told him, leaning one hip on the counter as she watched Austin pace her kitchen floor.

"You're right, and he will come around, once he's done making an ass of himself."

She knew he would eventually, but she wasn't going to wait forever. Well, she probably would, but no one needed to know that.

"Anyway, I came to tell you that I'm sorry." Facing her now, she could see so many emotions across his face.

"For what?" She drew her eyebrows together as she tried to work it all out.

"It took me a long time to really see Victoria for what she was, and I let her hurt you, our friendship, and so much else while I was blind."

"Oh, Austin, you don't have to apologize for that." She went to him, putting her arms around his neck in a hug.

"No, I really do." He brought his arms up to her back, hugging her as well. "I wanted you to know that I broke up with her."

She jerked away from him, keeping her hands on his shoulders as she looked up at him. "You did what?" Never in a million years did she think she would ever hear him say that.

"I called things off. I couldn't take it anymore, and every time she came around, it was like nails on a chalkboard. She wasn't going to change, so I knew what I needed to do."

"I'm so sorry, Austin." She was glad for it, but that wasn't going to ease his pain. Instead, she comforted her friend, hugging him again.

"What is going on in here?" Archer demanded from the entry to the kitchen.

12

"Archer!" Rachel jumped away from Austin.

He had walked in on them embracing in her kitchen, and it was a miracle he was still standing where he was. His body practically vibrated with the rage he was holding for both of them, but mostly Austin.

Staring at both of them, he tried to take a deep breath even as his fists clenched. It had been years since he'd really fought his brother, but right now, he was ready to do it now, though.

"Archer," Austin said cautiously, taking a step toward him.

"No, just no." Archer gritted his teeth, trying to hold it all in.

"Archer!" Rachel's tone was scolding. "What is wrong with you?"

He turned his focus solely to her. "What's wrong with me? You sleep with me and decide you need to see if the other twin was better?"

"Archer!" Austin yelled.

"Excuse me?" Rachel put her hands on her hips. "You did not just say that."

"Didn't I? Need me to repeat it, or are you trying to play innocent?" He was seeing red at this point and wasn't thinking about anything that came through his mouth as he spoke.

"Archer!" Austin yelled again. "What the hell is wrong with you?"

"You are!" he answered. "I told you I was having a hard time with everything, so you thought you'd come here and see if she's interested in you too?" He let out a sarcastic laugh, "Well, I guess you found out your answer."

"Don't you dare come into my house and accuse me of such a thing. Especially after you pretty much screwed me and ghosted!" Rachel yelled and stepped toward him. "Not that it's any of your business, but I was giving my friend a hug because he just broke up with his girlfriend and nothing else."

His brain couldn't process her words immediately, and he continued to glare at her.

"I will not have you belittle either of us that way. Besides, you pretty much already told me with your inaction how much you regretted our night, so what do you care?"

"Rachel," Archer said as he finally understood what she was saying.

"I'm going to leave." Austin looked between the two of them.

Rachel stepped in his path. "You do not have to leave." She turned back to set her glare on Archer, and he expected her to tell him to leave right then.

"I'm not going to deal with him right now, Rachel. We can talk later."

Rachel stepped out of his way, and Austin walked toward

him to leave. He expected Austin to just walk past him, but didn't expect the shoulder check Austin gave him as he walked past.

That was what broke the final thread that was barely holding his anger back. "Let me see you out," Archer said, turning around and putting a hand on Austin's shoulder and squeezing, practically pushing him out the door.

Austin, for his part, kept his mouth shut as they walked out, waiting until they were outside before he yanked his shoulder away from Archer.

"You need to go in there and apologize to her, and attempt to fix your mess, not be out here trying to fight with me." Austin folded his arms across his chest and raised an eyebrow at Archer.

"Then you should have just left." Archer folded his arms and raised his eyebrow back at him, a mirror image of his brother. "And you shouldn't have ran into me on the way out!" He was yelling but didn't care who heard.

"Bring it on, then. Let's see if you can still get Rachel to talk to you after you start a fight in her front yard and accuse her of sleeping around," Austin threw back at him.

When Archer didn't move, Austin spun on his heel and headed for his car. It took Archer a minute to decide what to do. He followed Austin to his car.

"What was I supposed to think?" he growled.

"You didn't need to think anything. You might have just asked." Austin yanked his door open as Archer reached him, slamming it into Archer. "I'm sorry! That was genuinely an accident."

"Yeah, I bet it was."

Rachel had apparently been watching the exchange and came running down her driveway to the road where Austin had parked on the curb. "What the hell, Austin?" she scolded.

"It was actually an accident; I didn't know he was so close." Austin tore his gaze from Archer to Rachel and back.

Archer's knee stung where the door had hit him, but it had knocked the edge off his anger. He knew when Austin was lying, and now that he was cooling off, he could confidently say Austin hadn't lied at all since he'd gotten there.

He also knew that Austin and Victoria had broken up, so he understood why he was here; he just hadn't expected them to be hugging. It was partially his own fault as well, or maybe mostly, since it had taken him a week to come to the realization about how he really felt about Rachel.

"I don't know what's going on, but either stay or go." She cut her eyes from him to Austin. "You are not going to fight in my front yard!"

"I'm going," Austin said, sliding into his car and shutting the door.

Rachel gave him a nod and looked at Archer. "Well?"

"I'm sorry," he started, "I came to say that anyway."

"I am not doing this in front of all my neighbors, Archer." She looked around to see if anyone was watching.

"I can come back if that's better, maybe try again." He should probably go buy her a whole florist's shop at this point before he came back.

"Fine." Rachel threw her arms up, letting them fall back down to her sides. She stormed back to her driveway before she yelped and took a knee. "Ouch!"

He rushed to her, and Austin climbed back out of his car. "Are you okay?" Archer crouched beside her at the entrance to her driveway.

"I stepped on something," she said, taking quick breaths.

Looking down, he urged her to sit so he could look at

her foot. Sure enough, blood was coming from the bottom of her left foot.

"What happened?" Austin asked as he closed in on them.

"Get the door." Archer leaned over and cradled Rachel as he picked her up to carry her inside.

She grabbed onto his neck as he carried her, and he took the opportunity to place a kiss on the top of her head. "It's going to be fine," he whispered.

"The counter," she told him as they went inside.

He carried her into the kitchen, careful to not bump any of the walls. Setting her down on the counter with her foot in the sink, he lifted the injured foot to take a closer look.

"It's cut pretty deep," Austin said from over his shoulder.

She hissed as he turned the water on and grabbed a clean towel from the drawer to hold to it.

"I know. We need to see how bad it is," he soothed as he worked, blotting at the cut, trying to see how bad it was. "I'm trying to be as quick as I can."

She nodded and leaned her head back, squeezing her eyes shut.

"I don't think it's that bad," Archer decided, "but I can take you to the doctor if you want to be sure."

"No, just need a bandage." Rachel looked at him with tears in her eyes.

"I'll get them." Austin jumped at the chance to leave the kitchen.

"Rachel, I'm so sorry." Archer held her foot with his left hand and reached up to stroke her hair with his other. He meant it for everything, her foot, his behavior today and all week.

"It's okay," Rachel whispered.

Austin got back with her small first aid kit, and Archer

tore it open looking for a good-sized bandage. Finding the one he wanted, he opened it up and inspected her foot again, noting that the bleeding was just an ooze now, a good sign. With all his work with metal in the studio, he'd injured himself more than once, and had learned how to recognize what was an emergency and what wasn't.

"I'm going to actually leave now, okay?" Austin asked from behind him.

"Okay," Rachel answered, keeping her eyes on Archer's face.

He reached around, lifting her up again, carrying her to the living room. Setting her down, he pulled one of her throw pillows from the couch and lifted her foot, placing it under.

"Keep that foot raised," he instructed.

"Are you leaving?" she asked, picking at invisible lint on her shirt, not looking his direction.

"Do you want me to?" He was scared she'd say yes, but would leave if that's what she wanted.

"I want you to decide what it is you want, Arch."

"I did. I came here to tell you, to let you know that I knew I was a jerk and that I wanted to try to make us work if you were even still interested."

"I'm still interested, but only if you're all in. You can't do this to me again and expect me to wait around for you, Archer."

"I wouldn't expect you to." He meant it.

"Then, please stay."

"Anything for you."

DON'T LEAVE
AUSTIN'S STORY TEASER CHAPTER

"What are your plans for Christmas?" Rachel, his brother's girlfriend asked.

"I don't know," Austin answered her; he hadn't made any decisions.

Six months ago he ended things with his long-term girlfriend at the same time that Rachel and Archer had started dating. Before that Archer and Austin had both been friends with Rachel for as long as he could remember.

The dynamic changed when they started dating though, and Rachel was still his friend, but it was different. She was around all the time, though Victoria, his ex-girlfriend, had kept her away with snide remarks and lots of attitude.

Austin looked over at his brother, Archer, a mirror image of himself aside from the tattoos and the smile. He rarely smiled anymore, and he knew it. He'd made a lot of headway in his career, though, throwing himself into work after breaking up with Victoria.

He stood and ran his hand through his sandy-blond hair. It was too much with the holidays coming, and he needed a break. If only his father, whom he worked for, would see it that way.

"Let us know soon?" Rachel asked.

"I will." He left them there in the living room and headed for his office.

Rachel wanted to host a Christmas party here at his and Austin's house, and he wasn't upset about it, but he wasn't feeling a party mood either. Everything was off, and he wasn't sure how he fit into anything anymore.

Overall, that was the biggest issue. He hadn't been as close with Archer for years, not really since he started dating Victoria and let her manipulate his relationships with anyone else.

He sat in front of his computer and pulled his emails. There were several event invites still sitting in his inbox that his father wanted him to attend, a few from his mother, on top of work meetings.

"Screw it," he said to all of it. Declining all the invitations he had, he cleared his calendar for two weeks overlapping Christmas through New Year's. He didn't have it in him to fake his way through the holidays.

In a new window, he looked for a secluded place to stay for that time; getting away might help him clear his head. There were very few options to choose from since he was looking for a place to stay in less than a week, over a holiday.

After searching multiple sites, he found one cabin to rent for the time he needed. Before he could debate it, he pulled out his credit card and made the reservation.

It was a three-hour drive away, but he was definitely going to tell his father it was further. Just thinking of the man had his phone lighting up.

"This is Austin," he answered.

"I need you to explain to me why you just declined all of my invitations." His father's voice was gruff, as it always was. He never had a nice thing to say.

"I'm taking off for the holidays and getting away for a few weeks." Austin did his best to keep his voice neutral and not give away how excited he was growing about his trip.

"You can't just do that!"

"You said yourself today that we are pretty much done for the year. I can wrap anything else up in the next few days."

"I was relying on you to help with our new clients."

His father had been pushing him to date the daughter of a big financial account owner that they were trying to land. Austin had refused several times. He wasn't like that and wasn't about to start acting like his father.

"I have already told you that I am not doing business that way."

"You want to run this company one day, then you're going to have to set that little moral code of yours to the side and get things done." A bang came through the phone, and he knew it was his father slamming his fist on his desk.

"And I've told you that I will not, ever. Once again, if you have a problem with the way I work, then you can let me go. I will step aside without a fight." This was sure to anger him further as it always did, but tonight he didn't feel like placating.

"That's not what I said!" The yelling had turned into a full-blown roar. "You will be here for those parties; there is no excuse."

"I need a break, and I will not be there. Do with that information what you must. I will be back after the New Year."

Ending the call, Austin stood, stretching his six-foot-four

frame as he did. He'd spent too long at a desk over the last several months. He'd take his computer, but resolved to not check on work.

If he ever managed to take over his father's financial firm, things were going to change, and he knew that scared some people and made others thrilled. He didn't care. He wasn't about to work 24-7 for the rest of his life. He didn't want that.

A small smile crept across his face as he thought about his trip. He only had a few days before he left, so he went to pack. He should have planned to leave tomorrow and just skipped the rest of work. He had enough work ethic to wrap up his own loose ends before he left, though.

Tomorrow would be interesting, his first meeting was sure to be with his father, and it promised to be loud. He could handle it, but he really didn't want to.

Before heading to his room, he stopped at the living room to let Rachel and Archer know of his plans. They were both very happy for him, or seemed it anyway. Archer had even patted him on the back for making the decision to take time off. He hadn't expected that.

Now, to get packing and make his escape for Christmas. He didn't hate the season; he just didn't want to deal with it this year. This was going to be better for everyone, and he was going to feel a lot better next year when he got back.

ALSO BY TONI DENISE

Learn More at tonidenisebooks.com

Westbeach Series:

Old Friends

On the Run

One Last Chance

Out of Time

Finding Love Series

Engaged to Her Neighbor

Married to the Playboy

Falling for Her Fake Husband

Short and Steamy Duet

The Wedding Date

The Wedding Ruse

ALSO BY TONI DENISE

Stone Twins Duet:

Please Stay (this book)

Don't Leave

(Don't Leave is included in the "Mine This Winter" collection available Dec 1, 2022)

Billionaire Blind Dates:

Jake